The Adventures of the Glo-worm Family

– CHARLES STEVENSON –

Illustrated by Nick Homfray

To Lynn, You Big Glo-Worm

C.W. St

An environmentally friendly book printed and bound in England by
www.printondemand-worldwide.com

FSC

Mixed Sources
Product group from well-managed
forests, and other controlled sources
www.fsc.org Cert no. TT-COC-002641
© 1996 Forest Stewardship Council

PEFC

PEFC Certified
This product is
from sustainably
managed forests
and controlled
sources
www.pefc.org
PEFC/16-33-415

This book is made entirely of chain-of-custody materials

First published 2012 by Fast-Print Publishing of Peterborough, England.

http://www.fast-print.net/bookshop

The Adventures of the Glo-worm Family
Copyright © Charles Stevenson 2012

ISBN 978-178035-333-8

First published 2012 by
FASTPRINT PUBLISHING
Peterborough, England.

To my three grandchildren:

Christopher, Saxon and Janey-Heather

Chapter 1
The Glo-Worm Family

The Glo-worm family's correct surname was, to be truthful, Lyte, but everyone who had ever known them always called them by their first names.

Papa Lyte was always known to everyone in the village as Edd and Mama Lyte as Florence.

Together, Mama and Papa Lyte had five young children whose names were Zun, Fan, Dip, Spot and Star.

The last two were lovely young baby twins, a boy and a girl.

The eldest boy, known as Zun, was the clever, brainy one of the family.

He was able to help his dad with anything that ever needed to be done.

He could mend or fix almost anything that needed to be fixed, especially when he had to help his dad to repair things that required their most urgent and immediate attention.

These were special things, such as when their boat needed to be repaired so that they could go out fishing, or the even more urgent everyday things, such as hunting or collecting food for the rest of the family to eat.

Fan was the eldest of the girls and her favourite job was to help her mum to do the things that girls and mums always needed to do, such as keeping the house clean or helping to cook extra-special meals.

She was the one that her friends had nicknamed "the cool kid" or "the arty one", because she loved to draw or paint pictures of anything that she had seen or done.

Dip was the younger of the two brothers and, of course, the mischievous one of the family.

He was forever getting into the kind of trouble that little boys always seem to get themselves into.

The two young twins named Spot and Star were the favourites of the family and, of course, the favourites of all of their friends and the neighbouring villagers.

The twins could do nothing wrong to anybody or anything.

Whatever they did or wanted to do, they would always be forgiven for it and allowed to get away with it time and time again.

It didn't matter how bad or how troublesome it could have been to anyone or anything, they were the favourite babies of the family and of all the other insects in the village, too.

The twins were always being spoilt by the Glo-worm family's friends and, of course, all the other village insects, because they loved them so much.

They were even able to keep their next door neighbour, Grumpy Grasshopper, happy after he became hopping mad when mischievous Dip flew over him at night with his body lights switched on too brightly.

This situation began to trouble Mama and Papa Lyte, who began to imagine that the twins might start to become the envy of all the other children in the family, especially as they were being spoilt so much.

But Mama and Papa Lyte didn't have to worry too much, as the older children seemed to have no trouble in keeping both the twins in complete check and under their absolute control.

Chapter 2

The Glo-Worms' Family House

The Glo-worm family lived high up in the trunk of a gnarled old oak tree in the comfort of an old abandoned woodpecker's nest hole.

The friendly woodpecker had abandoned its nest the previous year and had told the Glo-worm family that he wouldn't need it anymore and that they were welcome to use it for as long as they wanted to.

This was a truly generous gesture from the woodpecker and, after Mama Florence and Papa Edd had spent a short time cleaning the place up, they had now happily settled down to bring the rest of their family over from their old home, which was back in the swampy reed bed area, where they were continually being washed out by torrential rains that came thundering down every year.

This new house was the perfect place for them to live as it was high up in the tree with no chance of their ever getting flooded out or being washed away in any kind of storm or bad weather.

Mama and Papa Lyte would happily sit outside their front door holding the twins, Spot and Star, safely on their laps while the other children all played together, flitting and flying from branch to branch.

They could sit and watch mischievous Dip swinging on his rope ladder and, as the night grew darker, the children would sometimes play hide–and–seek, jumping from branch to branch whilst at the same time switching their tail lights off and on as they hid behind the tree's large green leaves.

It was only when Mama Florence shouted for them to come in and to tell them that it was time for them to go to bed that they would eventually have to finish their game and do as Mama Florence told them.

She would then tuck them safely into their tree house beds for the night and then she and Papa Lyte would spend the rest of the evening sitting there quietly planning for the family's activities for the next day.

Chapter 3

The Adventure Begins

The first adventure began when the Glo-worm family were out on the high seas aboard their own little sailing boat, the Nana-Leaf.

They were all happily enjoying the day sailing the clean, warm waters of their insect village's local sandy beach bay.

The family, consisting of Mama and Papa Lyte along with their five young children were always happy and content, fishing and swimming in the lovely clear waters when the sun was nice and warm.

The bay itself was situated in a faraway place on the coast of Africa where the Glo-worm family had all been born and had grown up.

They had lived there all of their lives and they were all happy, and contented to be away from the hustle and bustle of the other parts of the world that they had heard so many bad and fearsome stories about.

In this, their own special insect world, they lived in a place where they were always surrounded by other happy and friendly insects.

The kind of insects that would never have a bad word to say about any of the other insects that lived alongside them.

The Glo-worm family spent the vast majority of their days eating, fishing and generally lazing about in the warm and sometimes very hot sunny weather that prevailed in this part of the world. The village where they lived was aptly named Sleepy Hollow and they spent their days enjoying this quiet type of lifestyle.

The family never had to worry about getting anything to eat or drink as everything they wanted was found right on their doorstep, with enough food and drink to satisfy everybody in this quiet insect village.

Chapter 4
The Storm

Everything was going well, and the children were happily swimming and enjoying the warm, cool clear waters of the sandy bay.

They were also enjoying the plentiful supply of juicy titbits that Mama Florence had brought with her to keep them happy and content while out sailing on the boat.

The problems started when Papa Edd suddenly looked up from Nana-Leaf's deck and saw a heavy cloud formation that was building up on the far distant horizon.

He began to get worried as the clouds got nearer and nearer to where they were anchored.

Papa Edd had to make an instant decision.

"We had better make haste and get back to the shore as quickly as possible," he called out to his family, "or we will all get caught in the oncoming storm." At Papa Edd's sudden outburst, Mama Florence immediately ordered her children to climb back onto Nana-Leaf for their own safety.

"We must hurry and get ourselves back to the village as quickly as possible," she ordered, "before we find ourselves in a lot of trouble."

The warning shouts came too late.

The storm came quicker than they had all expected and Papa Edd could not save Nana-Leaf from being caught head-first into the stormy winds and the soaking downpour of rain that suddenly engulfed their tiny boat.

They were driven by the raging wind far out into the open sea that had so quickly turned from peacefully calm water into what was now a raging torrent of giant waves and rushing winds.

The storm could easily sink poor Nana-Leaf if Papa Edd didn't do something very quickly.

Chapter 5
Swept Out To Sea

Papa Edd and Zun had to take over the boat's steering wheel while Dip climbed onto the front of Nana-Leaf's bow and gripped tightly onto the mast's front sailing ropes.

He knew he was in danger of falling overboard if he didn't hang on for dear life, but he also knew how important it was for him to become the boat's lookout and to see if he could keep the distant fading land insight.

All chances of this were quickly washed away as the tiny boat was swept further and further out into the raging unknown of the now dark, deep-blue ocean.

To be truthful, none of the Glo-worm family had ever been this far away from their home village before. Mama Florence and her daughter Fan frantically struggled to keep the twins Spot and Star safely wrapped in their arms as Papa Edd and Zun struggled to keep the little boat Nana-Leaf on an even keel and safe from sinking.

The boat and the Glo-worm family were swiftly swept further and further out into the raging expanse of the ocean, while the storm still roared and blew on as it swept them further out to sea.

Mama Florence and Fan, holding tightly onto the two twins, had to hang on to the boat's sides for all they were worth, as they feared that they could be swept overboard and lost forever.

They began to realise that they were now completely and totally lost, as the boat with all of them on board was being swept further away from their comfortable tree-top home.

Mama Florence and daughter Fan tried harder and harder to keep the twins safe and warm by lighting up their bodies for extra warmth as they snuggled lower and lower down into the bottom of the boat whilst wrapping their arms around each other.

They had to protect themselves and the twins from any harm that the storm might throw at them, whilst still hoping and praying that the storm would soon be over and blow itself out.

All this time, Papa Edd and Zun, with Dip still hanging onto the mast's ropes, fought bravely to try to keep the tiny boat on a straight and even course and save from them all sinking.

Chapter 6
Land Ahoy! Land Ahoy!

The storm raged and blew all night long, but as it slowly passed them by, the sun, as if by magic, suddenly started to appear between the clouds and, before they knew what was happening, the weather changed.

The sun finally broke through the clouds and reappeared with a warm friendly glow, making once again for a brand new day.

The day finally changed from a once-frightening experience to a now-friendly morning again.

The wind and rain now began to drop and the Glo-worm family were at last able to believe that they might be over the worst of the past day's nightmare.

They began to hope and pray that now they would now be able to get their breath back and get onto safe and solid ground once more.

Dip was still clinging on tightly to the boat's mast, while still hanging on with his other hand to the front sail rope.

He had managed to stay there throughout the night's terrible storm without falling overboard. Mama Florence looked around and was so happy to see that he and the rest of her family were all still safe and sound on their little boat.

Dip hurriedly found his fishing bag and reached into it where he had put his fancy pair of binoculars.

He quickly grabbed them and began searching the horizon.

His eyes scanned carefully across the open ocean to see if he could see any signs of land, or even any other boats that might be in sight.

He was concerned and wondering where their tiny boat had been blown to.

His eyes searched from one side of the horizon to the other, but could see nothing of any sign of land or of other boats.

The hours slowly ticked by without Dip or any of the rest of the family able to see anything but the rolling of the waves as they broke into small and frothy bubbles over the surface of the sea.

The sun was now becoming hotter and hotter as it rose slowly, higher and higher above the horizon and started to burn their still wet and weary bodies.

The hours dragged on and on and Papa Edd and Mama Florence were becoming more and more worried that they might never see the safety of their tree home ever again.

It was getting late into the afternoon and Mama Florence was worried about how to feed the children before she had to get them into bed to get a little bit of rest and well-earned sleep.

It was at that very moment that Dip let out an excited shout. He almost deafened the rest of the family with his loud shouting.

"Land Ahoy, Land Ahoy," he screamed, "I can see a speck of land over there."

"Where? Where?" Papa Edd shouted back at him, "Where can you see land?"

Dip pointed wildly with his outstretched arm.

"Over there," he shouted back, "over there, over there."

Chapter 7
Nearly There

Papa Edd scanned the horizon to where Dip was pointing and, sure enough, there was the speck of land that Dip had eventually seen.

He quickly grabbed the boat's steering wheel and carefully turned Nana-Leaf in the direction in which Dip had sighted the tiny speck of land.

As they approached closer to the shoreline, they could see the waves breaking over the rough, outstretched rocks that seemed to surround any sign of a safe place where they could try to get Nana-Leaf on to any piece of solid ground.

Papa Edd urgently shouted to Dip to look out for a place where he could find any sign of a sandy beach, or some kind of safe cove where they could land Nana-Leaf without too much trouble and without hitting the rocks.

Dip carefully searched with his binoculars up and down the shoreline of the island, scanning carefully from the left-hand side of the island to its far right-hand side.

At long last he spotted a small sandy inlet, tucked between two outlets of jagged, surf-splashed rocks that were being sprayed gently by the ocean waves.

"Over there" he pointed wildly, waving with excitement, "Over there, between those outstretched rocks," he shouted back to Papa Edd.

Papa Edd spun Nana-Leaf's wheel onto a new course and gently sailed their little boat safely into a calm cove with a clean, yellow, sandy beach set between the jagged rocks.

Chapter 8
Solid Ground At Last

As the boat came to a grinding halt on the sandy beach, Dip quickly pulled the step ladder from under the boat's floor boards where it had been stored and pushed it over the side.

He scrambled overboard, laughing with excitement as he climbed down the ladder, landing safely on the soft, yellow, sandy beach.

"Come on down," he exclaimed with excitement, "come on down, we are safe at last."

Papa Edd followed Dip over the boat's side, making sure that all was safe and sound before he eventually turned and helped Mama Florence and the rest of the children down onto the sandy beach.

"Safe at last!" smiled Mama Florence as she stood holding her twin babies, Spot and Star, securely in her folded arms.

Brainy Zun and his sister followed Mama Florence and jumped down from the boat and, swaying unsteadily, trod warily over the sand onto their new landing place.

"This looks a quiet and safe place for us to stay and rest," Papa Edd declared.

"It's got to be much better than the place where we have been staying for the last few days anyway," he explained, in a rather nervous squeaky voice, "Anywhere must be better than where we have spent the last few days."

Chapter 9
A New House Must Be Found

"Our next problem," Mama Florence announced, with a touch of sternness in her voice, "is where are we supposed to live? We can't just sleep here on the sandy beach.

We need somewhere where it's safe and warm, where we are protected from any bad storms or rough seas that may blow up and surprise us at any time.

We have the children to look after and food to find," she explained to Papa Edd, with a worried look on her face.

"We need a new house to live in."

Papa Edd stood motionless, scratching his weary head with a sigh of despair.

"What do you suggest?" he asked, with a slight note of annoyance in his voice.

Dip was the first to react, "I will find a cave, he called out, with a sense of adventure in his voice.

"We can all live in a warm cave where I can explore and find things to do and play with all sorts of new friends."

"Not on your life," shouted Fan, "We must build ourselves a nice cosy grass house where I can plant some pretty flowers and paint my pictures and have a garden swing to swing on and be able to sunbathe in the daytime."

Zun, wasn't going to be left out of this conversation.

"We must find a large oak tree and build ourselves a new home like the last one we had," he declared with a certain amount of finality in his voice.

"I will go and surely find a tree that is big enough."

Papa Edd was still scratching his tired head while trying to listen to all the family's suggestions.

Mama Florence had been quietly listening to all these suggestions with a certain amount of patience and displeasure.

"Stop all of your arguing and fighting," she threatened them all, with a stern look on her face, "I will tell you all where I want to live and what kind of house we will all live in.

Now sit yourselves down on the sand while I get the twins fed and then I will tell you what I want done."

They all did as Mama Florence had instructed and sat down quietly until she had finished feeding the twins.

"What do you want us to do?" asked Papa Edd quietly, when he thought she was ready at last.

Mama Florence slowly turned her head from one side to the other as she surveyed the long, wide, open, sandy beach with no sign of any suitable trees or caves anywhere to be seen.

"There are plenty of stones and rocks around," she announced, "We must build a house that is strong and tall like the old oak tree where we used to live.

It must be round, with windows and a doorway where we can sit out and enjoy the kids at play.

It must be built high, away from any rough seas with a place on the rooftop so that we can watch for any passing ships or boats that might sail by.

It must be safe and warm with enough room for everybody to live in without getting in each other's way.

It must have a nice kitchen where I can cook the food and it must have a warm bedroom with a rocking chair where I can sit back, relax and put my weary feet up."

"You're not asking for much," exclaimed Papa Edd.

"How do you imagine we are going to build a house like that?"

Mama Florence stood motionless, "There will be no more arguing or complaining," she stated with a no-nonsense note in her voice.

"That is what I want and that is what I will get," she announced.

"You can all work out how you will do it, but I want it done and as quickly as you can."

Papa Edd was now in a quandary.

"What are we going to do now?" he asked the two elder boys, with a look of despair in his eyes.

Zun, the brains of the family, was the first to open his mouth.

"We must collect as many stones and rocks as we can find," he suggested, "bring them to the top of the beach and pile them as high as we can.

Then we must do as Mama Florence has said and build a round house as tall as any oak tree that has ever grown.

We must work all night long and, with the help of our glowing tails to see by, I'm sure we can build a new house for Mama.

If we all work together, we could have it built in no time at all."

Papa Edd thought carefully before he answered.

"Are you sure we will be able to do it?" he questioned the two boys.

"I'm sure we can," they both answered together, nodding their heads with excitement at the thought of all the hard work they knew they were going to do.

"Come on then," Papa Edd said, "let's get started.

It won't get done by standing here talking and complaining.

Let's get going!"

Chapter 10
The Finishing Touch

All through the night, Papa Edd and the two boys worked. The boys were busy fetching as many stones and rocks as they could collect for Papa Edd to build with.

Slowly but surely, the house grew, getting taller and taller as they worked hour after hour through the long night.

Mama Florence and Fan were kept busy keeping the two twins happy and quiet as they fed them and got them ready to go to bed under the shade of a lonely palm tree.

It was early in the morning that Mama Florence awoke to find that Fan had disappeared.

She looked everywhere, up and down the beach, but couldn't see her anywhere.

After gathering the twins into her arms, she raced off to find Papa Edd and tell him what had happened.

Papa Edd and the two boys were still busy building the house.

It had now grown so high that she thought that it would surely touch the bottom of the clouds.

There was still no sign of her daughter Fan, but Papa Edd told her not to worry and to help him and the boys with getting the house finished.

Mama Florence was not too happy with Papa Edd's answer, but she knew that all-hands-on-deck was the top priority and that the house needed to be finished before anything else was done.

The twins even helped with the building as they brought up wet sand in their sandcastle buckets to fill in any gaps or holes that were left between the stones and the rocks that Papa Edd had laid.

The day wore slowly on and the Glo-worm family were getting more and more exhausted, but the house, bit by bit, began to take its final shape.

After many more hours of seemingly endless work, Papa Edd finally stood back and announced to the family that the house was finished.

He decided there and then that enough was enough and that they should all now relax and admire all their hard work.

Mama Florence sat down on a smooth rock to take a satisfactory look at her new house.

"There is something missing," she declared.

"We need something else, we need a special name for our new house."

It was at that exact minute that Fan came into view, dragging a large lump of driftwood she had found on the beach.

She had found it wedged into the rocks, left there by the high tide and, as the tide turned and went out, she had managed to collect it.

She had known that the building of the house was not her kind of job; her kind of job was to draw and paint things, so she had slipped the piece of wood under her arm and taken it into the long grass.

She finally spread it on the ground to show all the family what she had been doing.

The sign said it all.

"This house is now named EDDY'S STONE LYTE HOUSE," she declared.

Mama Florence and Papa Edd, with the rest of the family, stood back to admire the new sign that Fan had painted for the new house.

They knew that between them all, the entire family had helped to build and that they would enjoy their new home for many more years to come.